hic,
hic,
hic

To Kiko
—M. C.

To Susan—my online savvy shopper who found
me the best bones
—S. D. S.

SIMON &
SCHUSTER

First published in Great Britain in 2002 by Simon & Schuster UK Ltd,
Africa House, 64-78 Kingsway, London WC2B 6AH.

Book design by Kristen Smith.
The text of this book is set in Caxton.
The illustrations are rendered in gouache, water colour and ink.
A CIP catalogue record for this book is available from the British Library upon request.

ISBN 0689 836716

Printed in Hong Kong

1 3 5 7 9 10 8 6 4 2

Skeleton hiccups

by margery cuyler

illustrated by S. D. schindler

Simon & Schuster

London   New York   Sydney

Skeleton woke up.

hic,
hic,
hic

Had the hiccups.   hic, hic, hic

Took a shower.

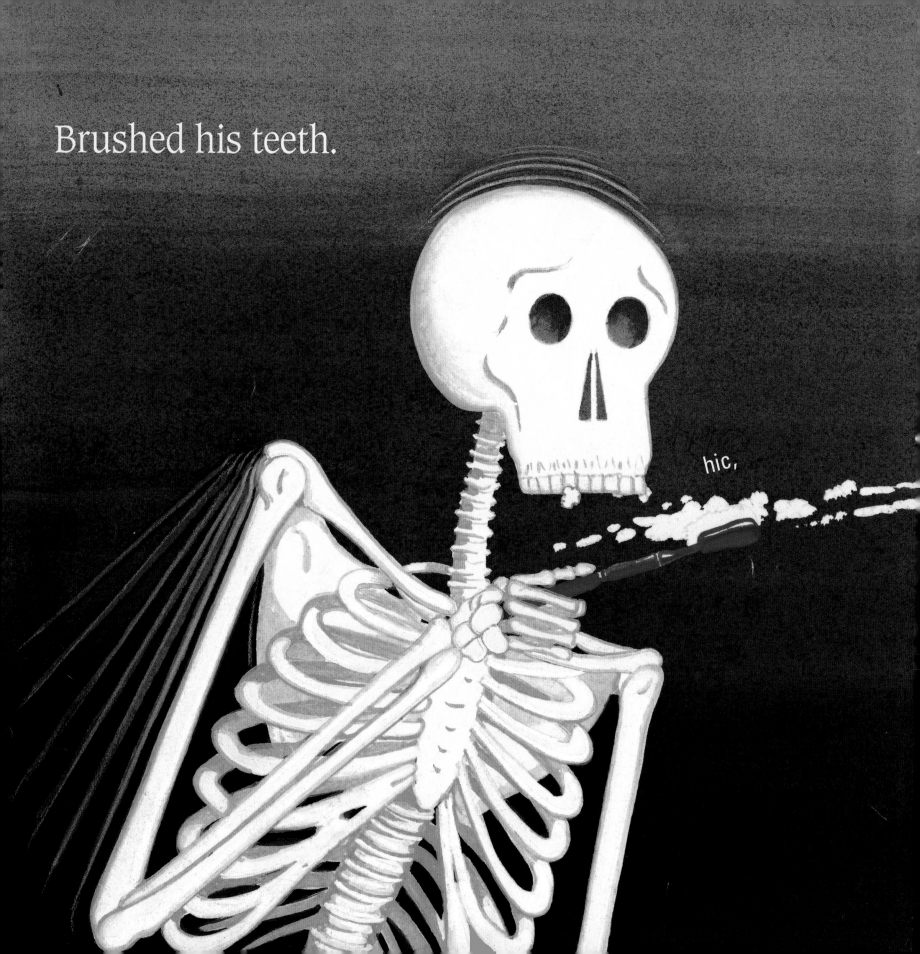

Brushed his teeth.

hic,

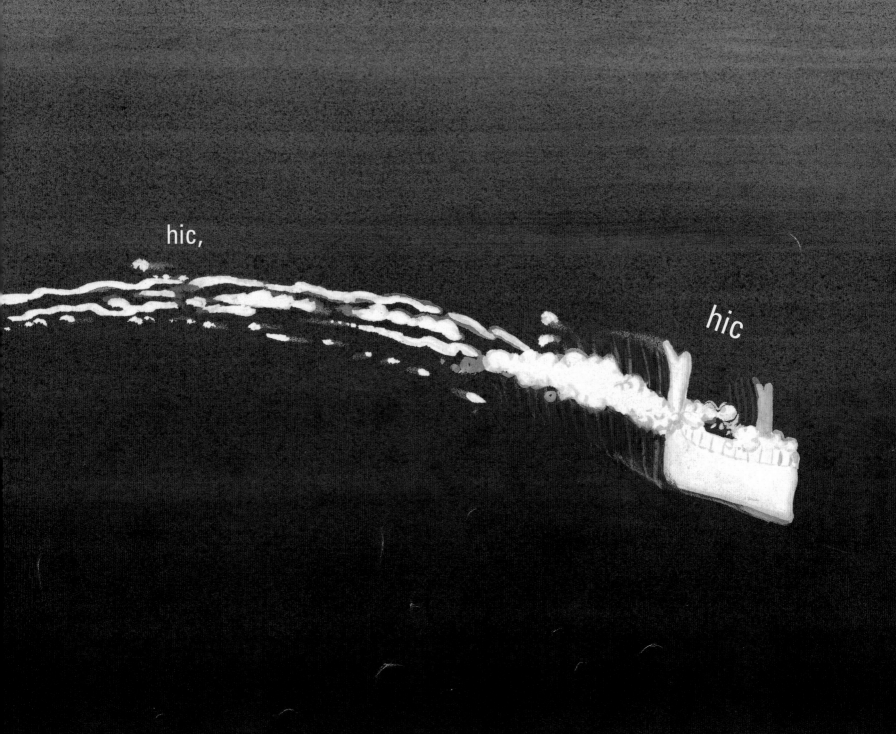

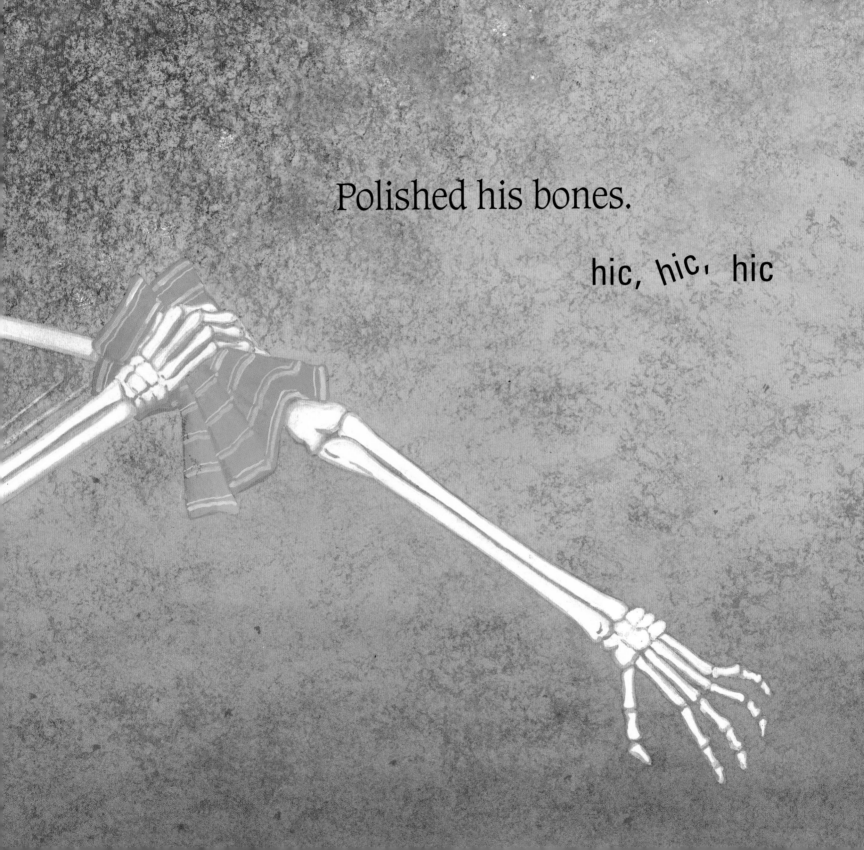

Polished his bones.

hic, hic, hic

Carved a pumpkin.

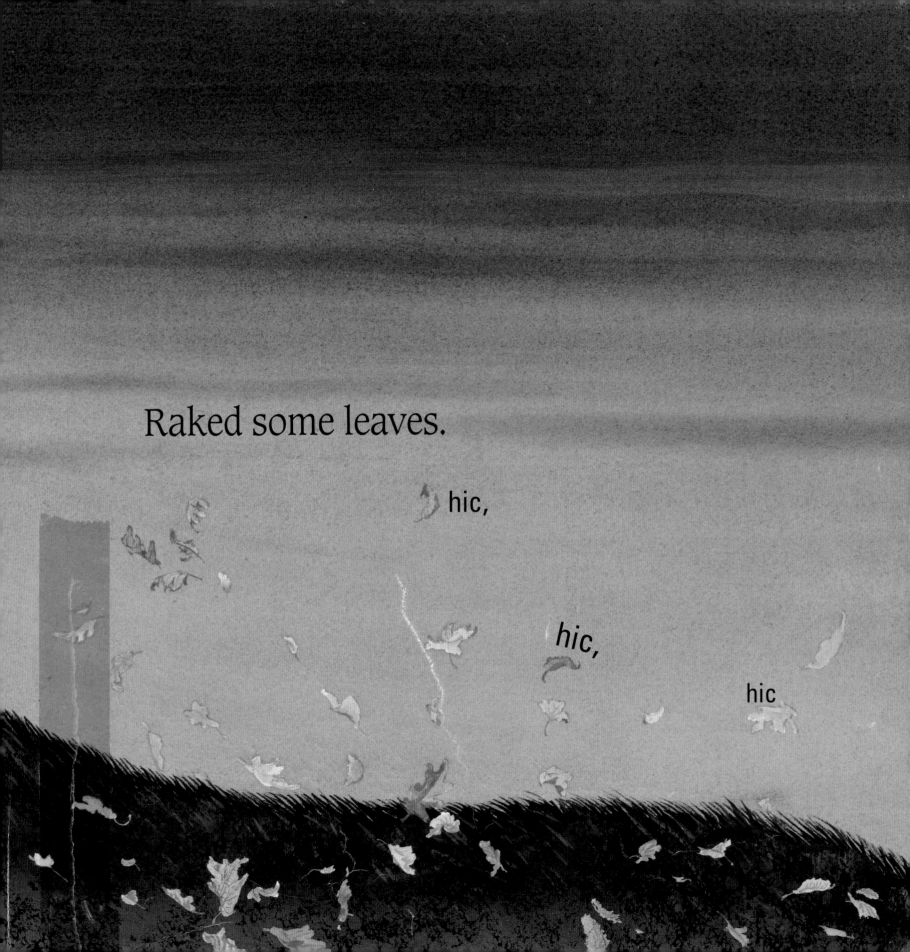

Raked some leaves.

hic,

hic,

hic

Played with Ghost.

hic,
hic,
hic

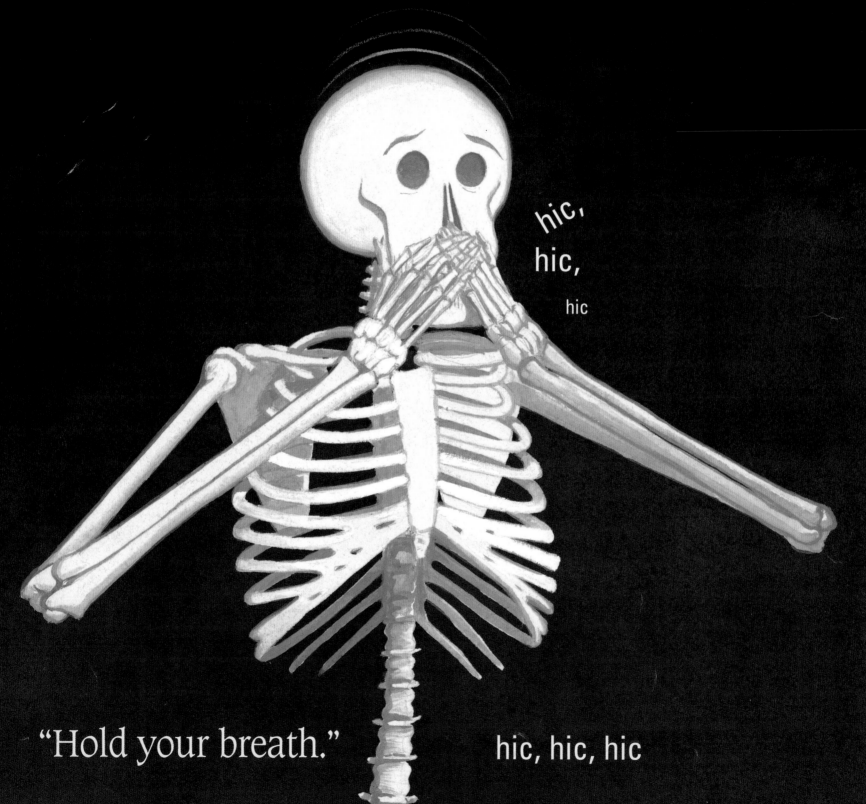

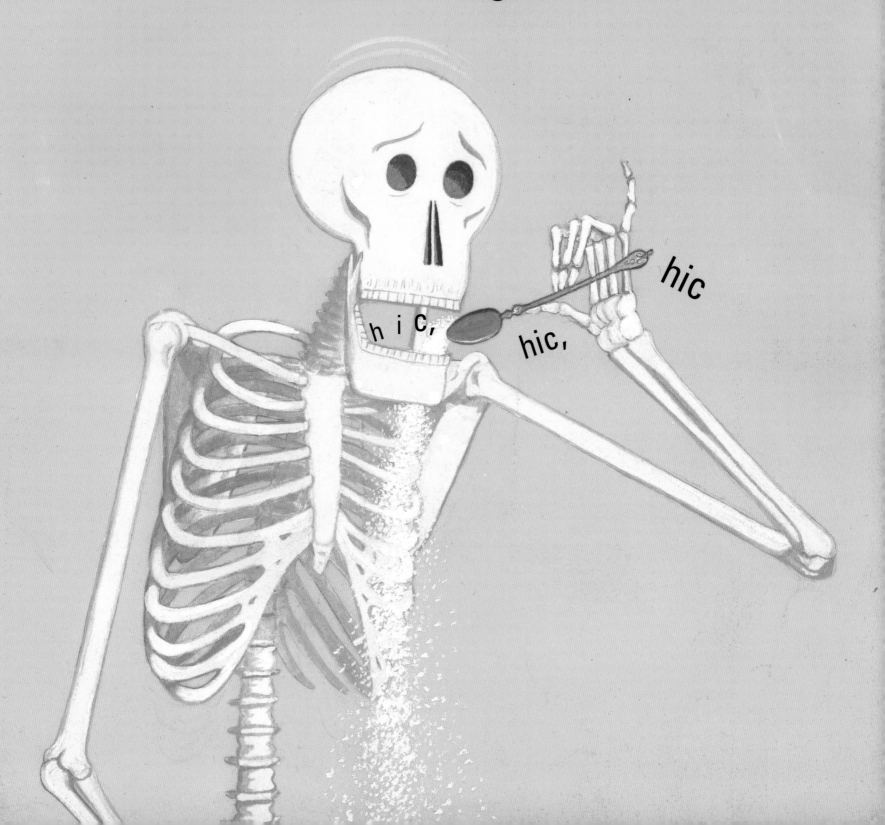

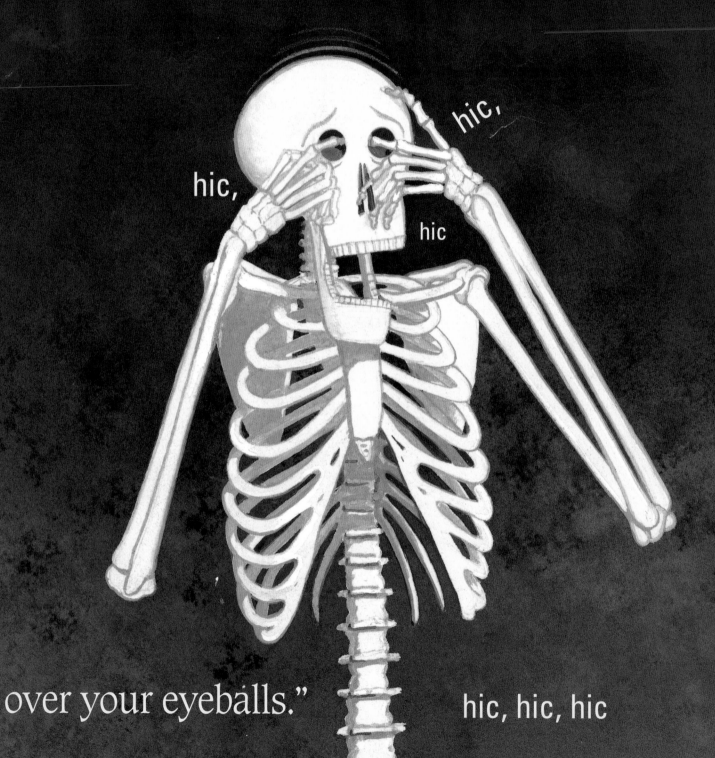

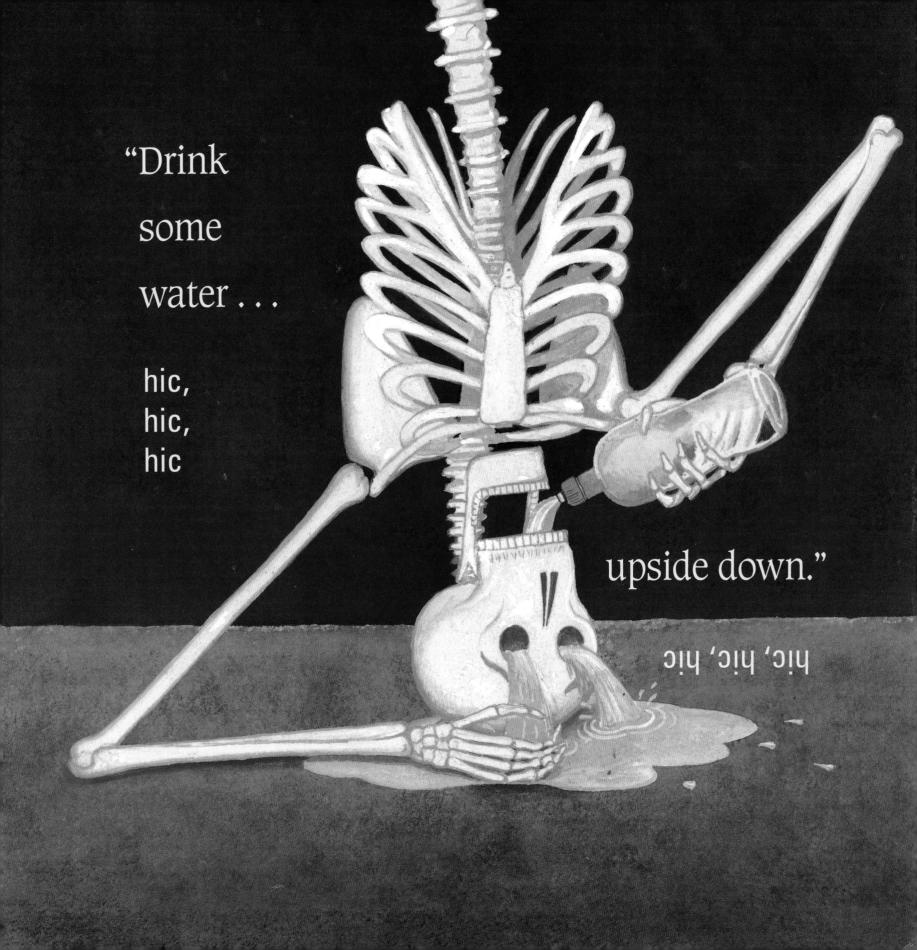

Ghost made a face.

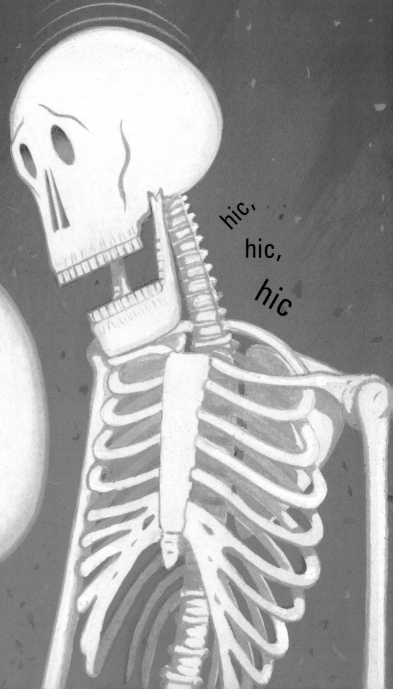

hic,
hic,
hic

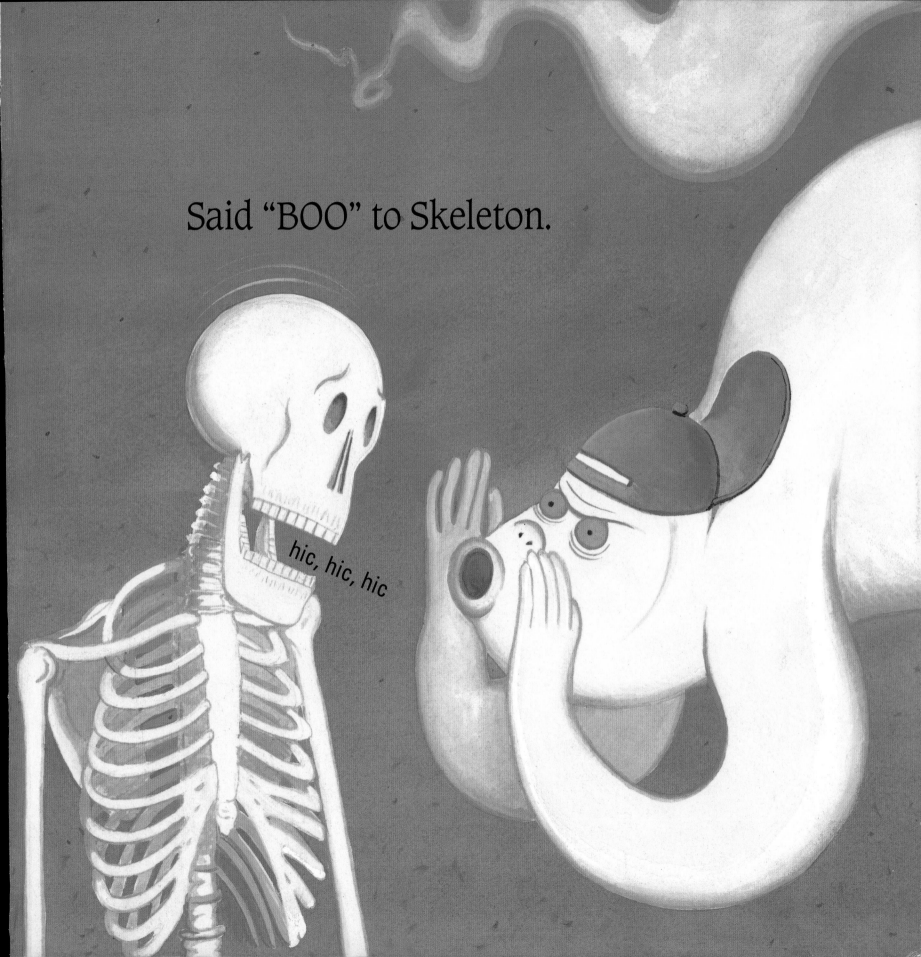

Said "BOO" to Skeleton.

hic, hic, hic

Then Ghost got clever.

hic, hic, hic

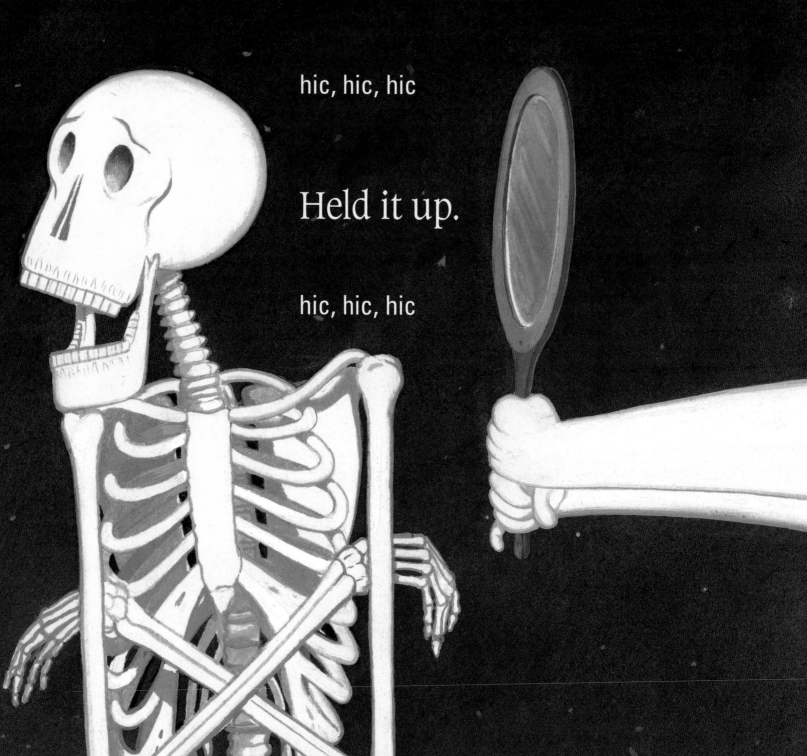

Found a mirror.

hic, hic, hic

Held it up.

hic, hic, hic

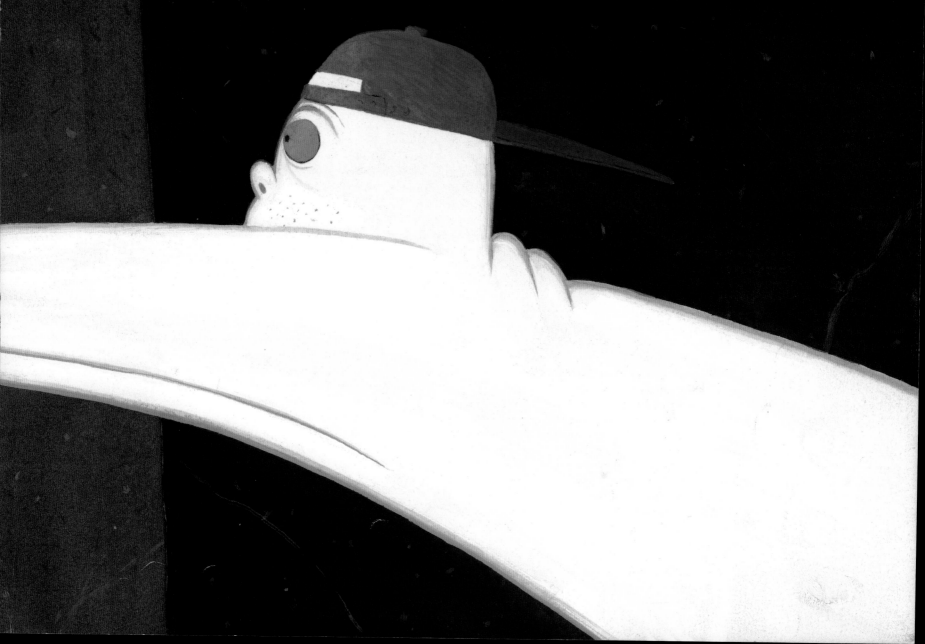

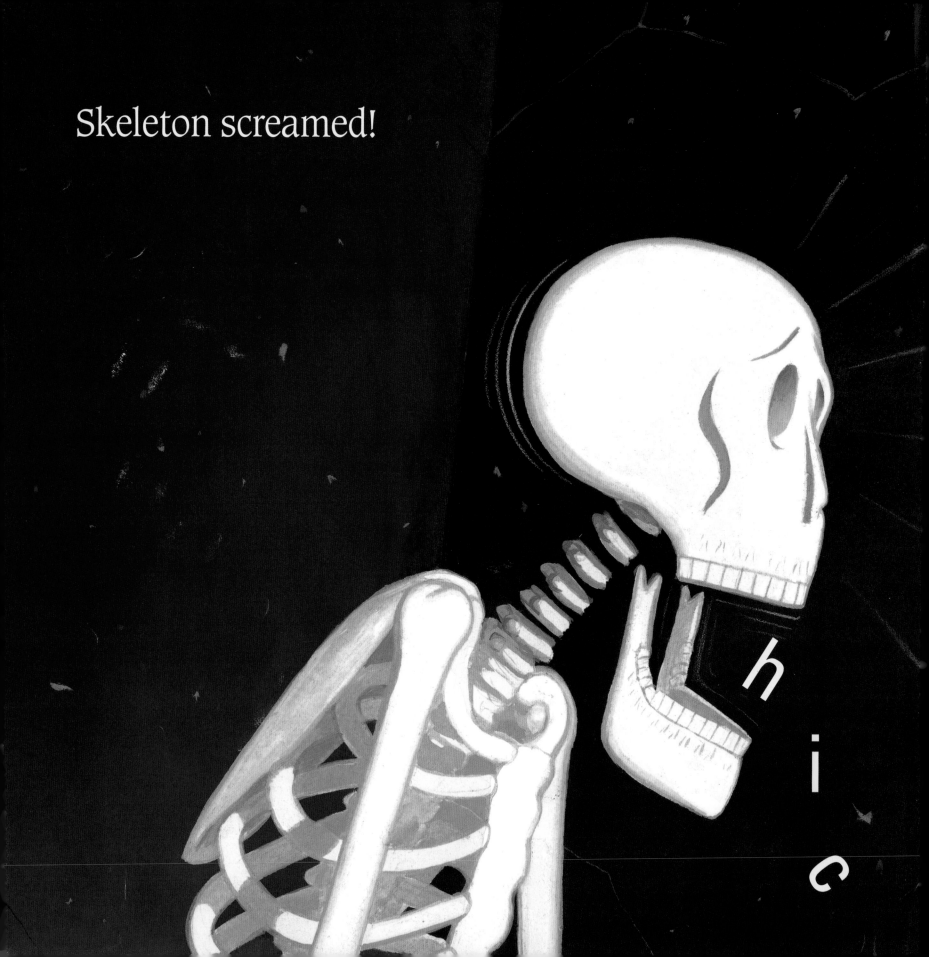

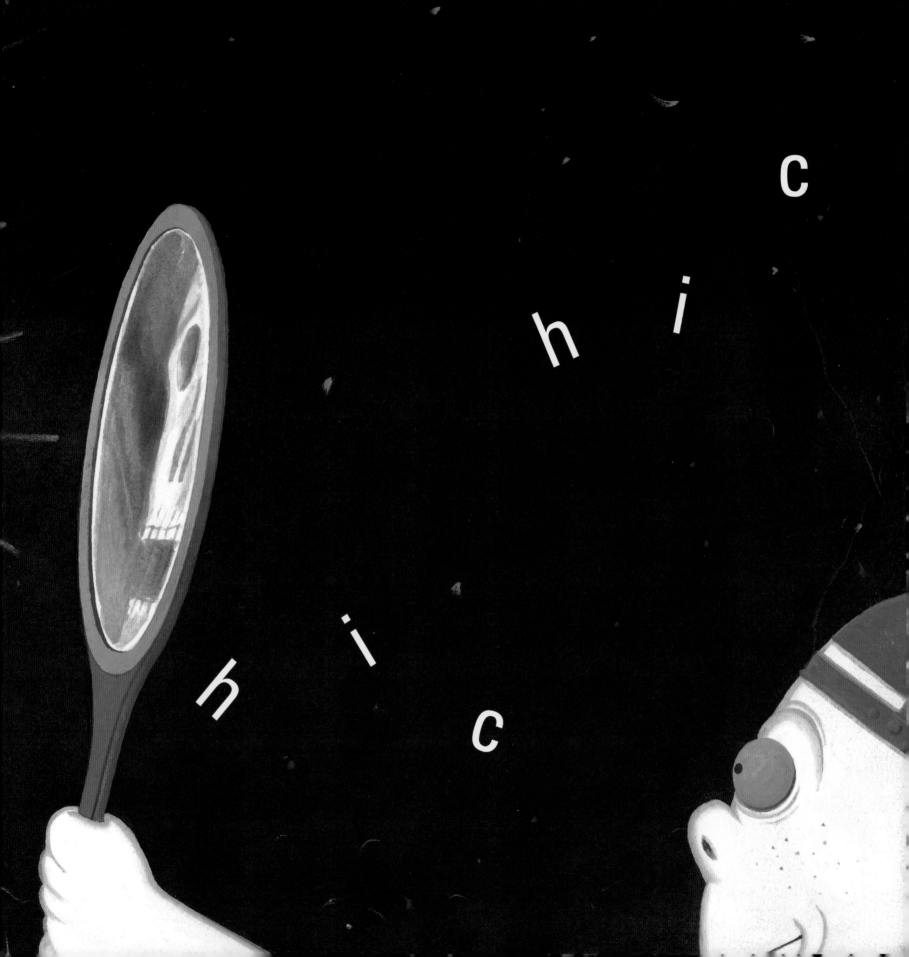

The hiccups left.

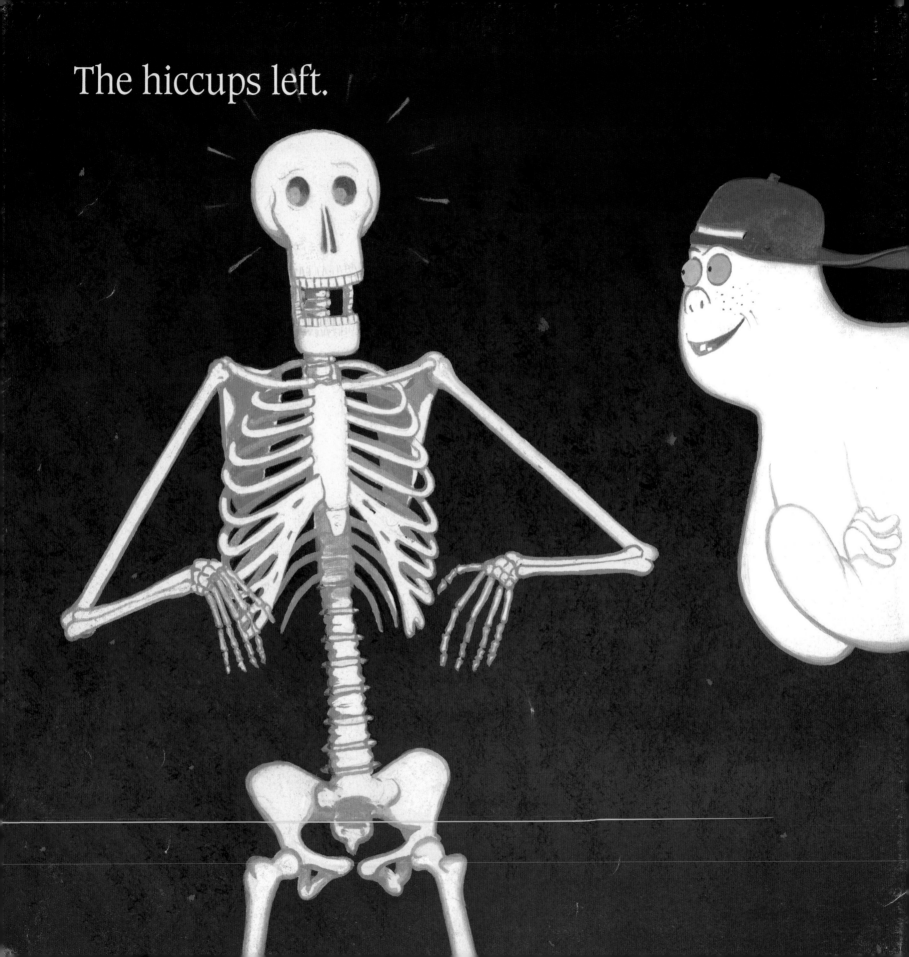

hic, hic, hic

They jumped away.

hic,

hic,

hic

Hooray!